**DO NOT REMOVE
CARDS FROM POCKET**

8-8-88

E

ALLEN COUNTY PUBLIC LIBRARY

FORT WAYNE, INDIANA 46802

You may return this book to any agency, branch,
or bookmobile of the Allen County Public Library.

FACE
THE MUSIC!

Make Me Laugh!

FACE THE MUSIC!

jokes about music

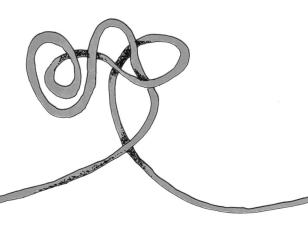

by Scott K. Peterson / pictures by Joan Hanson

Lerner Publications Company ✦ Minneapolis

To Anne Tekautz

Library of Congress Cataloging-in-Publication Data

Peterson, Scott K.
  Face the music!

  (Make me laugh!)
  Summary: A collection of jokes about music and
musicians, including "What do musicians brush their
teeth with? A tuba toothpaste" and "What's an
orchestra's favorite dessert? Cello."
  1. Music—Juvenile humor. 2. Wit and humor,
Juvenile. [1. Music—Wit and humor. 2. Jokes]
I. Hanson, Joan, ill. II. Title. III. Series.
PN6231.M85P48   1988   818'.5402   87-22657
ISBN 0-8225-0995-4 (lib. bdg.)

Manufactured in the United States of America

1 2 3 4 5 6 7 8 9 10 97 96 95 94 93 92 91 90 89 88

Q: How do fish practice their music?
A: With scales.

Q: Why wouldn't the bandleader go outside during an electrical storm?

A: Because he was a good conductor.

Q: Why did the director bring a baseball to the concert?

A: She wanted to have the right pitch.

Q: Why did the conductor hold the clock?

A: Because he wanted to make sure the orchestra could keep time.

Q: In what kind of show do cows sing?
A: A moo-sical.

Q: Why didn't the music students like their teacher?

A: Because she was too hot-tempoed.

Q: Why was the bass singer kicked out of music class?

A: Because he was always getting into treble.

Q: Why wouldn't the organist let the girls sing?

A: Because she wanted it to be a hymn.

Q: What do people sing underground?
A: Miner scales.

Q: Why can't secretaries hear concerts?
A: Because they take too many notes.

Q: Why did the singer go to the hospital?
A: She had to have an opera-ation.

Q: How do singers buy things?
A: With har-money.

Q: Why did the singer always carry a dictionary?
A: She didn't want to forget the words.

Q: What kind of singers do you find at Yellowstone Park?

A: Bear-itones.

Q: What kind of music do dieters like?
A: Slim-phonies.

Q: Why did the fiddler walk so strangely?
A: Because he was bowlegged.

Q: Why did the boy play his viola on a hill?
A: Because he was musically inclined.

Q: How do musicians sip drinks?
A: With orche-straws.

Q: What do you call a violin player who is riding a horse?

A: Fiddler on the hoof.

Q: What is an orchestra's favorite dessert?
A: Cello.

Q: Why did the bass player leave his girlfriend?
A: Because he didn't want any strings attached.

Q: Why did the boy write songs in bed?
A: Because he wanted to read sheet music.

Q: Why aren't lemons allowed to play music?
A: They make too many sour notes.

Q: Why did the trumpeter put an old towel in her horn?

A: She wanted to play ragtime.

Q: What instruments do skeletons like to play?

A: Trom-bones.

Q: What do musicians use to brush their teeth?

A: A tuba toothpaste.

Q: What did the musician eat on his birthday?

A: Flute-cake.

Q: Why didn't the drummer eat her carrots?
A: Because she liked her beats better.

Q: What happened to the drummer who bumped his head?
A: He got a percussion.

Q: Why did the boy quit his drum lessons?
A: Because he just couldn't stick with it.

Q: Why did the drums fall asleep?
A: Because they were beat.

Q: Why do drummers like rabbits so much?
A: Because they're easy to snare.

Q: Why did the man put sandpaper on his piano?

A: Because he wanted to be an organ grinder.

Q: How do piano players eat?

A: With tuning forks.

Q: Why couldn't the woman open her piano shop?

A: Because she forgot her keys.

Q: How does a musician make soup?
A: In a kettle drum.

Q: How do you clean the keys on a piano?
A: With Ivory soap.

Q: What kind of trousers do guitar players wear?
A: Chord-uroys.

Q: Why did the bass player want to weigh 300 pounds?
A: So he could play heavy rock.

Q: Why was the guitar so sad?

A: Because everybody was always picking on him.

Q: Why did the boy bring a stone to the bakery?

A: Because he wanted to see rock and rolls.

Q: Did you hear about the rock group called Cement?

A: It took them all night to set up.

Q: Why did the band go on a diet?

A: Because they wanted to play light rock.

Q: Why did the boy put a saxophone in the back of his car?

A: Because he wanted to jazz it up.

Q: Why didn't Mom go to the concert?
A: Because all they played was Pop music.

Q: Have you heard of a group called the Fishermen?
A: They aren't that bad, but they're always out of tuna.

Q: What's a bee's favorite song?
A: "I'm Stinging in the Rain."

Q: Did you hear that new song about eggs?
A: It's got a good beat to it.

Q: Why did the amplifier take speech lessons?
A: It wanted to be a better speaker.

Q: Why did the boy put his radio in the kitchen cupboard?
A: Because he wanted to dish-go.

Q: What did the disc jockey put on her car?
A: Radio tires.

Q: What do you call a record about hobos?
A: An al-bum.

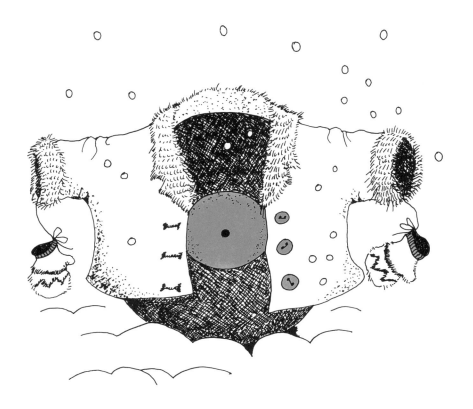

Q: How do records stay warm?
A: They keep their jackets on.

ABOUT THE AUTHOR

SCOTT K. PETERSON has always been able to make somebody laugh about something. A graduate of Coon Rapids High School, he has lived in Minnesota all of his life. He feels fortunate to have grown up in a family with a sense of humor like his and because of his love of music he met Anne Tekautz, to whom this book is dedicated.

ABOUT THE ARTIST

JOAN HANSON lives with her husband and two sons in Afton, Minnesota. Her distinctive, deliberately whimsical pen-and-ink drawings have illustrated more than 30 children's books. Hanson is also an accomplished weaver. A graduate of Carleton College, Hanson enjoys tennis, skiing, sailing, reading, traveling, and walking in the woods surrounding her home.

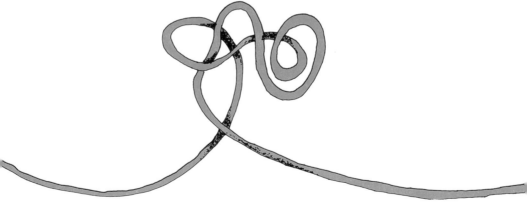

Make Me Laugh!

CAT'S OUT OF THE BAG!
DUMB CLUCKS!
ELEPHANTS NEVER FORGET!
FACE THE MUSIC!
GO HOG WILD!
GOING BUGGY!
GRIN AND BEAR IT!
IN THE DOGHOUSE!
LET'S CELEBRATE!
OUT TO LUNCH!
OUT TO PASTURE!
SNAKES ALIVE!

SOMETHING'S FISHY!
SPACE OUT!
STICK OUT YOUR TONGUE!
WHAT'S YOUR NAME?
WHAT'S YOUR NAME, AGAIN?
101 ANIMAL JOKES
101 FAMILY JOKES
101 KNOCK-KNOCK JOKES
101 MONSTER JOKES
101 SCHOOL JOKES
101 SPORTS JOKES